Text copyright © 1961 by Janet Charters
Reprint © 2010 by Janet Abis
Illustrations copyright © 1961 by Michael Foreman

Originally published in the U.K. in 1961 by Routledge and Kegan Paul Ltd.,
Broadway House, 68–74 Carter Lane, London, EC4
First published in the U.S. by Dutton Children's Books

First Templar Books/Candlewick Press edition 2010

Library of Congress Cataloging-in-Publication Data is available.
Library of Congress Catalog Card Number 2009027800
ISBN 978-0-7636-4875-6

9 10 11 12 13 14 CCP 10 9 8 7 6 5 4 3 2 1

Printed in Shenzhen, Guangdong, China

This book was typeset in Baskerville.
The illustrations were done in watercolor and gouache on paper.

TEMPLAR BOOKS

an imprint of
Candlewick Press
99 Dover Street
Somerville, Massachusetts 02144
www.candlewick.com

The

Janet Charters
illustrated by Michael Foreman

General

templar books
an imprint of Candlewick Press

There was once a general.

His name was General Jodhpur. He wanted to be the most famous general in the world and to have his army admired by generals from all the other countries. And so he kept his soldiers busy cleaning their weapons, ironing their uniforms, and polishing their medals and boots.

Every morning very early, as soon as the sun was up, the soldiers had to be out on the parade grounds smartly dressed and ready to practice marching.

When they had finished marching, the soldiers divided into several groups. The cooks went to the kitchens to prepare the meals. The cavalry went to the stables to groom and feed the horses.

The other soldiers went to the rifle range to practice shooting,
and the officers made sure that the men did their jobs correctly.

In the evening, when the camp was quiet, General Jodhpur liked to sit up late and read about other generals and the famous battles their armies had won. How he longed for the day when he and his army would be so famous that a book would be written about them.

One Sunday morning, while General Jodhpur was riding in the country on his big white horse, a bright red fox ran across the path. The horse was so frightened that it reared up, threw the general to the ground, and galloped off into the forest.

General Jodhpur was not hurt. He landed on some soft grass. The grass was so soft and smelled so sweet that, to his surprise, the general found that he did not want to move. He picked a blade of grass, put it between his teeth, and lay back in the warm sunshine.

After a long time, he decided that he ought to be getting back to camp. Reluctantly he got to his feet and set off at a brisk march.

Although he had ridden along the path many times, he now noticed things he had never seen before because he was always going so fast. He saw squirrels and rabbits and field mice and hedgehogs and swallows and wood pigeons and even a peacock.

He heard the birds singing. All at once the general came upon a field of beautiful flowers. Never had he seen such a wonderful sight. There were more kinds of flowers than he had ever imagined and more colors than any artist had ever dreamed of.

General Jodhpur stood quite still for a few minutes, and then he slowly walked across the field and sat down in the middle of the flowers. He watched the bees buzzing in and out as they searched for pollen to make honey. He thought that one would be sure to land on his nose, but the bees were far too busy to notice even a famous general.

He watched the flowers and the bees for a long time. How peaceful it was. Why had he never noticed these things before?

When at length he got up, he was dismayed to see that he had been sitting on some of the flowers. They looked sad and droopy. He did not want to leave the flowers, but he had to get back to his soldiers. He decided to pick two flowers.

It was dark when General Jodhpur finally reached the camp. He put the two flowers in a glass of water near the window of his room and went to bed.

That night he dreamed about the wonderful things he had seen during the day — the birds, the animals, the sun, and the flowers. Then into his dream marched thousands of soldiers. They made such a dreadful noise that the birds and the animals fled in terror. The soldiers trampled the lovely flowers flat. The general woke up, furious. "Stop, stop!" he shouted at the soldiers. Then he realized that it was only a dream. He tried to go to sleep again, but he could not.

He knew that he and his soldiers must have marched over thousands of beautiful flowers and frightened small animals many times. "I will never harm or frighten anything again," he said to himself. "I will try to help the animals and tend the flowers and plants and all other things that grow."

In the morning he told the soldiers that he wanted them
to leave the army and return to their homes and jobs. He
wanted them to help him make their country the most beautiful
country in the world. Everyone was so happy. But nobody was
happier than General Jodhpur.

The farmers started to plow their fields and sow seeds for the next harvest.

The fishermen took their nets and went out to sea.

The general ordered the builders to turn the army camp into a lovely city

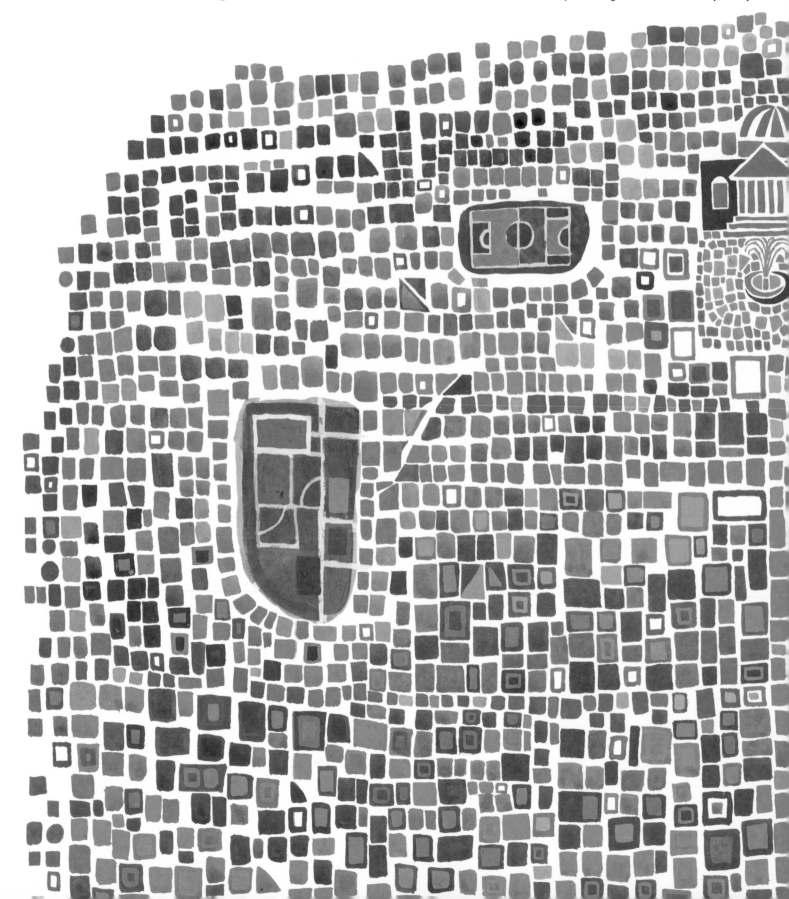

with shops and schools and to build parks where children could play.

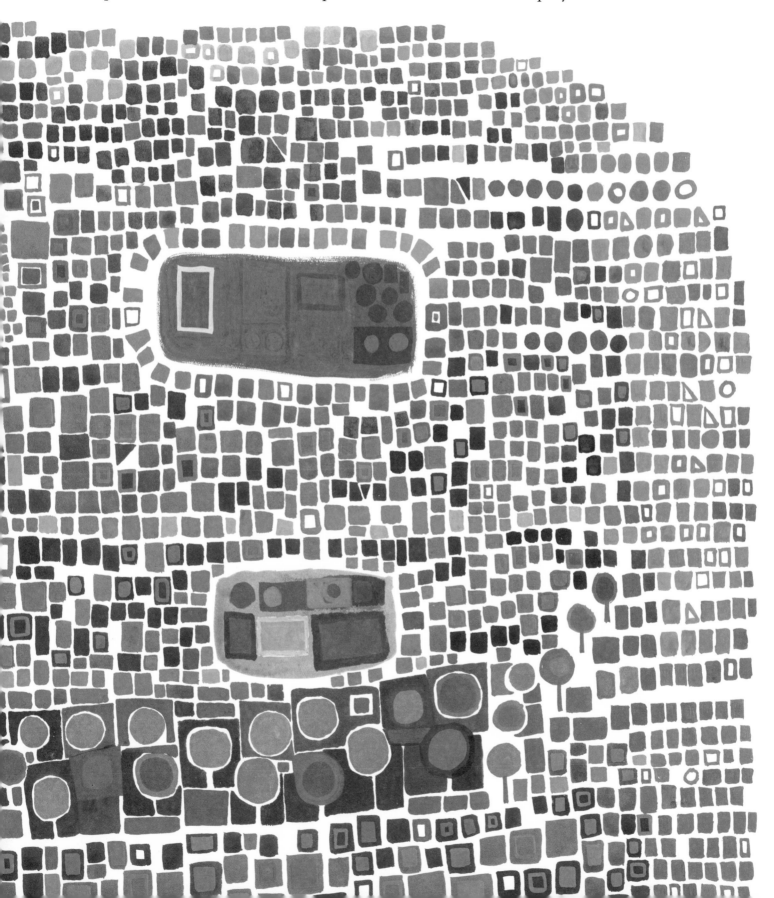

General Jodhpur was very excited by all that was happening. When he visited his men to see how their work was progressing — and he did so every day — they were glad to see him.

Each day he also went to
the place where he had
first seen the flowers. It
was wintertime now and
the flowers were no longer
there, but he liked to look
at the field where they had
been and to feel the earth
with his hands. He knew
the flowers would be back
in the springtime.

At last winter was gone. The flowers returned to the countryside.
New green leaves appeared on the trees; the seeds that the farmers
had sown began to thrust their shoots through the soil.

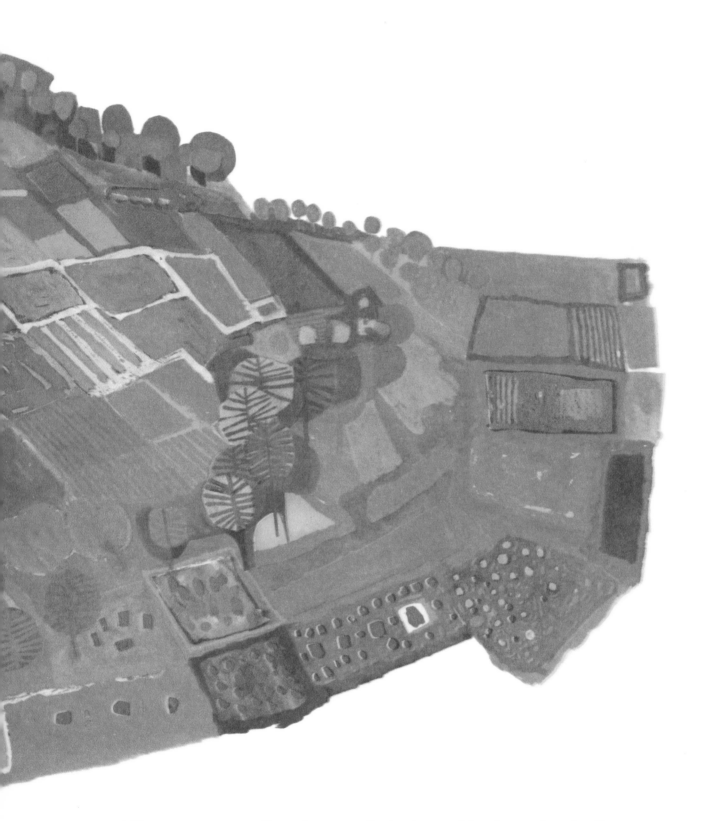

The corn grew tall and green; fruit ripened in the orchards. Every morning the fishermen sang as they took their boats out on the shining sea.

One morning General Jodhpur received two important-looking letters. One was from the famous General Nicolai Marcovitch, from the eastern part of the world. The other was from the equally famous General Custard, from the western part of the world. Both generals wanted to see for themselves the strange things that they had been told were happening in General Jodhpur's country.

General Jodhpur at once invited them to visit him and to inspect his country. When General Nicolai Marcovitch and General Custard arrived, they were greeted by General Jodhpur and a brass band. Then General Jodhpur proudly took the visitors all over his country.

He showed them the orchards and forests, the fields full
of vegetables and grain, and the fine city with its parks and
playgrounds. The visiting generals saw that the people

regarded all the animals as friends and never frightened or chased them. Finally, General Jodhpur took them to the place where he had first seen the flowers.

The fields for miles around seemed to be covered with a blanket of a million colors. The three generals sat down — carefully, so as not to damage any of the flowers — and smiled at one another. "This is a wonderful idea," said General Custard. "You have made your country the most beautiful in the world."

"And your people are certainly the happiest," added General
Nicolai Marcovitch. And together they said, "General Jodhpur,
you are the most famous general in the whole world."

And the Most Famous General in the Whole World lay back among the flowers and smiled at the sun.

PUBLISHER'S NOTE

Janet Charters (now Abis) was born in England in 1938, on the eve
of the Second World War. Growing up in the uncertain atmosphere
created by the Cold War and the nuclear arms race, Janet
developed an acute awareness of the fragility of peace.

Michael Foreman was also born in England in 1938. Having not
known a world without war, he thought that it was normal. One
frightful night while a three-year-old Michael lay fast asleep, a
bomb came crashing through his bedroom ceiling—this is his first
memory. The bomb missed him by a few inches, bounced on the
floor, hit the wall, and then dropped into the fireplace, where it
exploded up the chimney. When the war ended, Michael looked
forward to a world of peace, but unfortunately his teenage years
were lived under the threat of nuclear war.

In creating their first book, *The General,* Janet and Michael wanted
to produce a fun and lively story that encouraged a sympathetic
outlook on the world. Now, almost fifty years later, the book seems
even more relevant as not only the need for peace but also the
threat to the environment, hinted at in the story, are both now
clearly evident.